cloverleaf books™

Stories with Character

Bundle of Nerves
A Story of Courage

Mari Schuh

illustrated by **Natalia Moore**

MILLBROOK PRESS • MINNEAPOLIS

To the Martin County Library
—M.S.

For Terry, Andy, and Mike,
With Love, Natalia

Millbrook Press
A division of Lerner Publishing Group, Inc.
241 First Avenue North
Minneapolis, MN 55401 USA

For reading levels and more information, look up this title at
www.lernerbooks.com.

Main body text set in Slappy Inline 22/28.
Typeface provided by T26.

Library of Congress Cataloging-in-Publication Data

Names: Schuh, Mari C., 1975– author. | Moore, Natalia, 1986–
    illustrator.
Title: Bundle of nerves : a story of courage / by Mari Schuh ;
    illustrated by Natalia Moore.
Description: Minneapolis : Millbrook Press, [2018] | Summary:
    Luis is very nervous about the first day of school, but finds
    many ways to be brave. Includes an activity and glossary. |
    Includes bibliographical references and index.
Identifiers: LCCN 2017008882 (print) | LCCN 2017034387
    (ebook) | ISBN 9781512498219 (eb pdf) | ISBN 9781512486452
    (lb : alk. paper)
Subjects: | CYAC: Anxiety—Fiction. | Courage—Fiction. | First day
    of school—Fiction.
Classification: LCC PZ7.1.S33655 (ebook) | LCC PZ7.1.S33655
    Bun 2018 (print) | DDC [E]—dc23

LC record available at https://lccn.loc.gov/2017008882

Manufactured in the United States of America
1-43469-33209-7/12/2017

TABLE OF CONTENTS

Chapter One
So Very Nervous

Ring! Ring!

My alarm goes off.

Today is the first day of school!

My stomach feels funny. **I'm so nervous.**
My big brother says I'm a bundle of nerves.
I think he's right!

"What if my teacher calls on me?
What if I don't know what to do?"
Everyone might stare and laugh at me.
That would be so embarrassing!

Having courage is doing something that's hard to do, even though you're afraid.

Dad gives me a big hug at the bus stop.
"Have **courage**, Luis, and you'll do great," he says. "I bet you'll even have fun!"

Chapter Two

Being Brave

The bus pulls up, and I get on. It's almost full! There's a boy sitting by himself. "Can I sit with you?" I ask.

I think I made a new friend!

At school, I see lots of new people. I don't know anyone!

I'm going to have courage, just like Dad said. I decide to say hi to everyone. **It feels good!**

It takes courage to meet new people.

Uh-oh, I don't remember where my classroom is! My stomach feels funny again.

Wait a minute . . . I can ask for help!

It takes courage to
ask for help.

At recess, I see a girl playing alone.
She tells me her name is Kia.

"Want to play together?" I ask her.
"Let's join the big game!"

Chapter Three

Facing My Fear

Back in class, my teacher, Mr. Lund, wants a student to lead a sing-along.

What if he asks me?

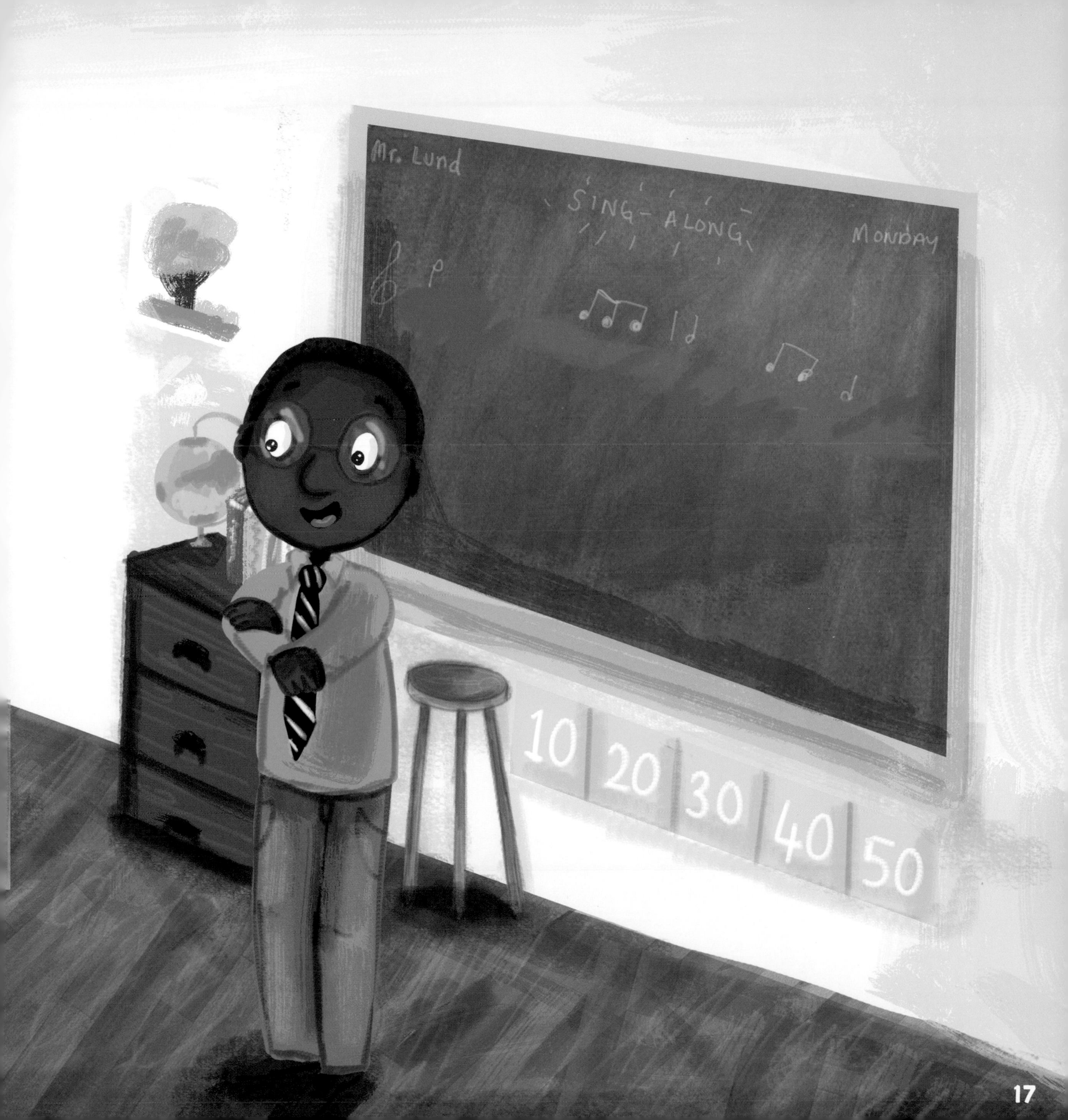
Mr. Lund
SING-ALONG
MONDAY
10
20
30
40
50

Then I remember I had a lot of courage today. I rode the bus, asked for help, and made new friends. **So I know I can do this too!**

I take a deep breath and say,
"I'll lead the sing-along!"

Dad was right. I had courage, and today ended up being lots of fun.

I think tomorrow will be fun too!

Make a Courage Calendar

When you think about it, you'll see you do many things that take courage!
Pay attention to things you do at home and at school. Before you go to bed,
think about your day. Did you do anything that took courage? Did you learn
something new? Or did you stand up for what you believe in?

Make your own courage calendar to keep track of what you do
that takes courage.

What You Will Need
a large monthly calendar
stars or stickers

What You Will Do
1) If you did something that takes courage today, find today's
   date on the calendar and put a star or a sticker on that date.

2) All month, think about your day before you go to bed. Put a
   star on the calendar if you used courage in any way.

3) At the end of the month, count all your stars. How many do
   you have? Maybe you will have even more stars next month!

GLOSSARY

bundle: a group of something

courage: the ability to bravely face hard tasks or situations

embarrassing: something that makes you feel foolish in front of others

nerves: feelings of being frightened or worried

nervous: worried about something

sing-along: a fun time when people sing songs together

BOOKS

Hanson, Anders. *Stand Up for Yourself: The Kids' Book of Courage.* Minneapolis: Abdo, 2015. Discover lots of different ways to show courage throughout your day.

McKee, David. *Elmer and the Monster.* Minneapolis: Andersen Press USA, 2014. Read about how an elephant named Elmer shows courage in the jungle.

Meiners, Cheri J. *Have Courage!* Minneapolis: Free Spirit, 2014. Read more about how to have courage at school and at home.

Schuh, Mari. *Yes I Can! A Story of Grit.* Minneapolis: Millbrook Press, 2018. Learn about another important quality to have—grit, which is the ability to keep working toward a goal no matter what.

WEBSITES

Courage
http://characterfirsteducation.com/c/curriculum-detail/2272029
Visit this website and watch the videos to learn more about courage.

Courage Crossword Puzzle
http://kidsandvalues.com/wp-content/uploads/2011/10/courage4.pdf
Work on this word search puzzle to learn ten ways to show courage in your life.